MAKING FRIENDS

BACK TO THE DRAWING BOARD

KRISTEN GUDSNUK

MAKING

BACK TO THE DRAWING

Graphix
An Imprint of
SCHOLASTIC

Library of Congress Control Number: 2019932098

ISBN 978-1-338-13927-3 (hardcover)
ISBN 978-1-338-13926-6 (paperback)

10 9 8 7 6 5 4 3 2 1   19 20 21 22 23

Printed in China   62
First edition, August 2019
Edited by Adam Rau
Book design by Phil Falco
Publisher: David Saylor

 To Kathryn.

WEREN'T THE REPAIRS SUPPOSED TO BE **DONE** BY NOW?

CAUTION DO NOT ENTER CAUTION CAUTION CAV

CAUTION

IT MIGHT TAKE THEM **YEARS** TO FIND FUNDING. THIS WAS PROBABLY **MILLIONS** OF DOLLARS OF DAMAGE.

EVERYONE IN CHEERLEADING HAS TO SELL FOUR BOXES OF GYM-REPAIR FUND-RAISING CHOCOLATES OR WE'RE OFF THE SQUAD.

CHOCOLATE, ANYONE?

rattle rattle

CHOCO

...AND WE'VE GOTTA ORGANIZE THE **SAVE MELTON DANCEATHON**.

A SCHOOL DANCE?!

THEY'RE ANNOUNCING IT TODAY. IT'S IN A WEEK OR SO.

100

CRUNCH

YOU'RE ALL COMING, I DON'T CARE WHO'S TOO COOL FOR DANCES, SO JUST ACCEPT IT.

GYM

WE'VE JUST GOTTA FIND A LOCATION, BECAUSE THE GYM IS A HAZARD ZONE.

CAUTION CAUTION

COUGH, COUGH. IF ONLY **SOME**ONE WOULD TAKE RESPONSIBILITY FOR THE GYM.

ME? HUH?

I...

2

TIP
TIPTIP

I TOOK CARE OF THAT ALREADY!

TALKIN' BOUT MY EDUCATION!

ANY DAY NOW, THEY'RE GONNA PROCESS THAT MONEY AND RELEASE SOME *GLOWING STATEMENT* ABOUT THEIR RICH ANONYMOUS DONOR.

sigh...

AAAANY DAY NOW...

MY GYM TEACHER HAS JUST BEEN SHOWING US VIDEOS ABOUT... PUBERTY-RELATED SUBJECTS.

WHICH MY PARENTS WON'T LET ME WATCH, ANYWAY. THEY WROTE A *NOTE*.

IT'S *SO EMBARRASSING!* I JUST WANNA PLAY SOME BADMINTON--AND NOT IN THE PARKING LOT, EITHER!

English

Les Sad
• French
• Sad
• No singing

WHAT THEME IS JON VAL JON EXPRESSING ON PAGE 142?

DANIELLE?

I THINK JABERT IS IN LOVE WITH JON VAL JON!

WHY ELSE WOULD HE FOLLOW HIM TO THE ENDS OF THE EARTH?

BUT HIS RIGID IDEOLOGY WON'T ALLOW HIM... TO ACCEPT HIMSELF!

AMOUR

BAGUETTE

I DREW SOME FAN ART OF THEM OPENING A FRENCH BAKERY TOGETHER...

What?

?

NO

BOOO

BOOOO

??

lotta spare time...

C'MON, READING IS FUN! IT'S LIKE WATCHING A MOVIE IN YOUR... MIND? UM... THAT IS...

SIT DOWN!

BOO READING SUCKS

THAT IS, UH, I'M SORRY, I MISSPOKE; READING IS LAME...

SORRY FOR THE INTERRUPTION...

Grammar is SERIOUS

mutter mutter...

4

DANIELLE, I'M DISAPPOINTED IN YOU!

I THOUGHT YOU WERE A LITERARY-MINDED YOUNG LADY.

I THINK READING IS FUN, MRS. LECTOR!

YOU'RE WONDERFUL, MADISON.

...CARA TOLD ME SHE LIKES TO READ.

SIGH

hm...

DON'T DRAG ME INTO... WHATEVER THIS IS.

yeah

CAN WE GET BACK TO LEARNING?

GOOD IDEA, CARA.

CHEER

WOO!

CLAP CLAP

clap clap

SHRINK

YEAH!!

6

7

HIGH 5!

AW, YEAH! TEAMWORK!

POM

UH, CONGRATS? DO YOU WANT A MEDAL?

no...

HARUKA KANATA

I TOTALLY LOBBED THAT BALL— YOU SAW?

...

10

...MRS. ROUGEAU IS **PREGNANT** AND SHE'S LETTING WHOEVER DOES BEST ON THE TEST **NAME** THE **BABY**!

I WANNA **WIN**!

WHAT IF IT'S YOU? WHAT WOULD YOU NAME THE BABY?

CLEOPATRA! COMIN' ATCHA!

...ANY NEW **SECRETS** YOU'RE **WITHHOLDING** FROM US TODAY, DANY?

heh...

WAIT, **REALLY**? I WAS JUST KIDDING. THE **WORLD** ISN'T IN DANGER, IS IT?

WHO DO WE GET TO FIGHT **THIS** TIME?

NAH, IT'S NOT LIKE THAT...

I JUST FOUND THIS NOTE IN MY LOCKER...

"YOU LOOK LIKE A *GLOWING ANGEL* TODAY."

I'M LIKE A CHRISTMAS TREE TOPPER!

YOU *DO* LOOK VERY DEWY TODAY.

AW, SHUCKS! THANKS, LEAH!

hmm

SUSPICIOUSLY DEWY.

LOOK! YOU'RE *LITERALLY GLOWING!* WHAT THE HECK!

FWIP

OALS: STUDY ARDER

BEEP BEEP

6:45 AM

UGHHH...

BEEP!!

WELL... I CAME UP WITH THIS HANDY MAGICAL LIFE HACK...

13

DINGG!

Reminder: History essay due

NOW YOU TELL ME?!

I told you yesterday too.

HISTORY ESSAY...

...THAT SEEMS LIKE I WROTE IT, BUT DID AN UNCHARACTERISTICALLY GOOD JOB.

SOMETHING THAT WILL MAKE MRS. MARKS...

...THINK I'M SMART.

POOF!

OH, AND MY MATH HOMEWORK TOO.

UGH. I'M SO TIRED.

SOLAR HEALING POWER. MAKE ME FEEL LIKE I'M NOT DYING.

WOMAN, YOU'RE MY WOMAN, I LOVED YOU ALL MY LIFE... ♪♫

GOD, DAD! LEARN ANOTHER SONG ALREADY!

LAUREN, THAT'S OUR WEDDING SONG... KEEP PLAYING, CHUCK.

EMPEROR CORN SYRUP LIL BITES CEREAL
yummy!

WHEN WE MET, WE DIDN'T KNOW, THE DOG DAYS WE HAD AHEAD— ♪♫

ha ha

MR. ROMANO, HUH? I HAD HIM. EASY A.

LAUREN! ARE YOU *KIDDING* ME?

IF YOU THINK PRE-ALGEBRA IS HARD... JUST WAIT FOR *ACTUAL* ALGEBRA. AND THEN PRECALC. AND CALC.

NOOO...

FIRST OUTER, INNER LAST. *FOIL.* IT'S SO EASY. I MISS WHEN MATH WAS EASY.

OH, YOU DEFINITELY MISSED THE BUS.

NO I DIDN'T! BYEEE!

DASH

LET ME KNOW IF YOU NEED A RIDE TO SCHOOL.

YOU'RE NOT GONNA EAT ANYTHING, LINDA?

I'M NOT HUNGRY.

FWOOSH

♪ ♫

HI, DANY!

TAP O' THE MARNIN' TO YA, TOM!

HUH?

U.H... "TOP OF THE MORNING TO YOU."

OH, YEAH. YOU TOO.

SO, DID YOU ALSO MISS THE BUS?

NOPE. FLYING IS JUST *SO* MUCH BETTER.

YEAH...

HEY, HOW COME NO ONE EVER NOTICES US *FLYING*? I THOUGHT I'D BE THE NEW *BIGFOOT* BY NOW. MELTON'S OWN FLYING BOY.

I THINK THE FLYING RINGS HAVE A CLOAKY SHIELD THINGY. IT WAS SOMEWHERE IN THE BACK OF MY MIND WHEN I DREW THEM.

WE'RE NOT *INVISIBLE*, BUT NO ONE WOULD EVER, LIKE, NOTICE US FLYING AROUND.

...I MEAN, WE CAN'T HAVE PEOPLE COMING AFTER US FOR OUR MAGIC!

WE'D HAVE TO FIGHT THE *GOVERNMENT*! THAT WOULD BE GNARLY!

GNARLY IN THE *BAD* WAY, MAYBE!

IT WOULD BE BOTH GNARLIES.

23

LIKE CHARGING MY LAPTOP...

...DOING HOUSEHOLD TASKS...

VRRRRRR

...YA KNOW, BASICALLY INVENTING NEW KINDS OF LAZY.

FLICK

...THAT'S WHAT THEY CALL "THE ROOT OF HUMAN INNOVATION."

WOW...

CAN YOU MAKE FIREWORKS WITH YOUR POWERS? YOU SHOULD DEFINITELY MAKE FIREWORKS.

OOH! I WONDER!

25

REALLY.

YEAH.

WAIT, BUT READ THIS ONE UP CLOSE—

"YOU'RE SWEAT AND GORGEOUS"?

WELL, HE GOT ONE PART RIGHT.

I THINK HE MEANT "SWEET."

SWEAT AND GORGEOUS!

BUT LIKE, *AM I* EVEN "SWEET"?

NORMAL

SIGH...

HE ALSO SAID, "YOU'RE THE ONLY ONE WHO SEES ME." SO I *MAY* BE COMMUNING WITH A GHOST.

SWEAT AND GORGEOUS!

I DON'T THINK I'D LIKE A BOY WHO CAN'T EVEN SPELL "SWEET."

EDWARD YANG ALMOST BEAT *ME* AT THE SPELLING BEE.

ULTIMATELY I DESTROYED HIM, OF COURSE.

WANT ME TO ASK HIM IF HE *LIKES* YOU?

YOU BETTER NOT!!!

26

OH, MADISON, I'M THINKING OF HAVING ALL THE GIRLS COME OVER THIS WEEKEND. WE CAN PRACTICE OUR ROUTINES...

I WAS TALKING TO COACH AND SHE SAID IF WE DON'T GET ENOUGH PRACTICE, WE WON'T MAKE IT ANYWHERE *NEAR* THE CHAMPIONSHIP. ARE YOU FREE?

yeah

GOOD IDEA! NOT GONNA LIE, I FORGOT HOW TO DO THE SCORPION.

DON'T DO THE SCORPION! YOU COULD GET STUNG!

HARDY HAR HAR.

WOW, DANY, YOU HAVE A HILARIOUS REPLY TO *EVERYTHING.*

TH... THAT'S ME!

WHAT IS *THAT* SUPPOSED TO MEAN?

SHE'S JUST ALWAYS *HERE.* CHUCKLING IT UP. IT'S *ANNOYING.* NO OFFENSE.

yeah

27

THAT'S SO RUDE.

BUT I *SAID* "NO OFFENSE"!

OH MY GOD, DANY CAN TAKE IT. RIGHT, DANY?

yeah

IT'S COOL, I'M COOL. I CAN GET ALONG WITH MY FELLOW CLASSMATES.

NORMAL

ANYWAY, MADISON, ARE YOU AROUND THIS WEEKEND?

YOU'RE A JERK. C'MON, DANY.

MADISON, WHY ARE YOU STARTING A FIGHT OUT OF NOTHING?

IT'S NOT *NOTHING!* SHE CAN'T TALK TO MY *BEST FRIEND* LIKE THAT! I'LL QUIT CHEERLEADING JUST TO *SPITE* HER.

I-IN HER DEFENSE, WHAT IS CARA SUPPOSED TO DO IF I ANNOY HER? JUST SILENTLY PUT UP WITH IT FOREVER?

WAIT, WHY ARE YOU ON *HER* SIDE?

IF SOME ANNOYING DORKY GIRL STARTED SITTING WITH ME AND INTERJECTING DUMB JOKEY COMMENTARY, I MIGHT WANT HER TO LEAVE ME ALONE TOO.

28

IT'S KINDA HARD TO BE ON YOUR SIDE WHEN **YOU'RE** NOT EVEN ON YOUR SIDE.

I'M SORRY...

MAYBE I'M OVERREACTING. MAYBE IT'S JUST MY **FRIENDSHIP PROGRAMMING** KICKING IN.

MADISON, YOU CAN'T JUST RAGE-QUIT **CHEERLEADING**! THAT WOULDN'T HELP **ANYONE.**

I CAN DO WHATEVER I **CHOOSE.**

CRAP! I LEFT MY BACKPACK IN THE CAFETERIA!

SEE YOU IN CLASS.

BRRING

NORMAL

??

WHO WOULD JUST... THROW AWAY MY BACKPACK...

TRASH

VEN D

TRASH

TO THINE OWN ELF BE TRUE

HONESTLY...

29

SMIFF...

I DON'T KNOW HOW YOU'VE *CONNED* MADISON INTO BEING YOUR *FRIEND.*

AND *ALEESHA* TOO. THEY'RE *MY* FRIENDS. YOU CAN'T JUST... *INSERT* YOURSELF.

I'M SORRY I'M ANNOYING. MY FRIENDS TOLD ME TO "BE MYSELF," AND I INEXPLICABLY LISTENED TO THEIR ADVICE.

YOU KNOW WHAT, IT'S ACTUALLY SWEET OF YOU TO APOLOGIZE.

BUT IT DOESN'T CHANGE THE FACT THAT YOU'RE-- LIKE, YOU'RE WEARING A SHIRT THAT SAYS "NORMAL"?

...I JUST THOUGHT IT WAS FUNNY.

IS THE JOKE THAT YOU'RE WEIRD?!

NORMAL

MADISON SAID SHE'D *QUIT CHEERLEADING* IF YOU DIDN'T APOLOGIZE TO ME. YOU DON'T HAVE TO--

ME? APOLOGIZE TO *YOU?* SO I CAN'T EVEN SAY WHAT I *THINK* ANYMORE?

I GUESS YOU WERE... *UNAWARE* OF MY EXTREMELY SENSITIVE FEELINGS--

SHE'D QUIT *CHEERLEADING* OVER SOMETHING THIS *STUPID?!*

LOOK, I DON'T WANT HER TO DO IT EITHER--

NO? WELL, IT SURE **SEEMS** LIKE MADISON DOES WHATEVER YOU SAY.

N-NO SHE DOESN'T!

WE CUT SARAHLEE FROM THE TEAM FOR MADISON. SARAHLEE EVEN HAD HER WIDDLE **MOMMY** CALL UP THE SCHOOL TO COMPLAIN ABOUT IT! (WHAT A LOSER!)

I COULD **RUIN** MADISON AT THIS SCHOOL, IF I WANTED TO.

I CAN RUIN YOU TOO, ALTHOUGH IT'S NOT LIKE YOU'VE GOT MUCH OF A REPUTATION TO KEEP OTHER THAN "LOCKER WHISPERER."

GEEZ, CARA!!! I'D **PAY** YOU NOT TO DO THAT.

RECOIL!

NORMAL

THAT WORKS FOR ME.

WAIT, REALLY?

DO YOU ACTUALLY **HAVE** ANY MONEY?

I DO! UHH, MY PARENTS WON THE LOTTO.

I'LL BUY **ALL** YOUR CHOCOLATES. THEN YOU'LL LIKE ME?

31

JUST **PRETEND** TO BE MY FRIEND WHEN MADISON'S AROUND!

SO, **THIS** IS HOW **YOU** MAKE FRIENDS?

heh

IS THAT WHY MADISON'S FRIENDS WITH YOU? IT'S FINALLY STARTING TO MAKE SENSE.

SLUMP

MADISON AND I ARE FRIENDS BECAUSE... WE JUST ARE.

CHOCO

SHE'S NOT, LIKE... INDEBTED TO ME OR ANYTHING.

COOL! I HAD NO IDEA YOU WERE RICH.

CHOCO

TODAY IS AWESOME!

NORMAL

Danielle,
you're the only
who sees me.

You are sweet
and gorgeous
— Secret
Admirer

BRRINGGG

...SO I'M WASHING OFF
MY BACKPACK, AND
CARA COMES IN.

UGH.
CARA.

YOU CAN'T BE MAD AT HER ANYMORE! SHE APOLOGIZED TO ME— SHE WAS SO NICE ABOUT IT—

REALLY?

YEAH! WELL, I JUST TOLD HER, LIKE, "YOU HURT MY FEELINGS. AND THAT'S NOT OKAY."

I'M PROUD OF YOU! YEAH, SHE NEEDS TO LEARN TO **RESPECT** YOU.

SHE WON'T DO IT IF **YOU'RE** APOLOGIZING TO **HER** WHEN **SHE'S** MEAN TO **YOU.**

...

ALL YOU NEED IS MORE TIME TOGETHER. JUST TO GET TO KNOW EACH OTHER.

I DUNNO ABOUT THAT.

CHOW

...YOU CAN HELP US ORGANIZE THE **SAVE MELTON DANCEATHON.**

...

I DON'T... UH...

I'LL CONVINCE THE BOTH OF YOU.

You can't talk to me like that!!

You're right! I'm SO sorry!

I can talk to you how I want! You wanna see mean? You haven't seen MEAN YET!!

no no no

MADISON!

You don't deserve to be Madison's friend!

LIAR!

You paid off Cara to be friends with you??

It backfired and I'm stealing your magic!

why am I thinking like this??

WELCOME

silence...

Anyone home?

NORMAL

Splendid Magic PERSONAL MEMOIR BY DANIELLE RADLE

ROUGH DRAFT

WHAT A TERRIBLE MEMOIR.

THUNK!

ROUGH DRAFT

I HATE THE MAIN CHARACTER.

FLOP

HAIR

35

HOW CAN I EVER GO BACK TO SCHOOL? AND PRETEND EVERYTHING IS FINE?

AND SIT WITH **CARA** AT LUNCH WHEN SHE **OOZES ANNOYANCE** AT MY **VERY EXISTENCE?**

AND IF I SIT WITH **TOM,** MADISON WILL KNOW CARA AND I DIDN'T REALLY MAKE UP.

AND I'LL BE LIKE, "I LIED? CARA HATES ME?"

AND THEN **MADISON** WILL HATE ME TOO.

AND WHAT IF SITTING WITH TOM IS ACTUALLY SECRETLY **ANNOYING** BUT HE'S TOO NICE TO SAY SO?

WHAT IF I'M ANNOYING **MADISON** AND **SHE'S** TOO NICE TO SAY SO?

WHAT IF THAT'S MY WHOLE LIFE FOREVER UNTIL I DIE?!

IF ONLY I HAD A CLONE.

IF I HAD A CLONE, SHE COULD SOLVE *ALL* MY PROBLEMS.

I will help!

BUT IF SHE'S ME, WOULDN'T SHE HAVE ALL THE SAME PROBLEMS?

NO! NOT IF I COULD... *IMPROVE* ON THE ORIGINAL.

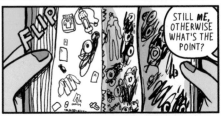

STILL *ME*, OTHERWISE WHAT'S THE POINT?

BUT LIKE... PERHAPS SOME CONFIDENCE. THAT'D BE NICE. WHAT A CONCEPT.

OOH!

SHE COULD BE...

SECRETLY...

A *PIKKIMAL!* SO I KEEP HER IN A PIKKIBALL WHEN SHE'S NOT IN USE. THAT WAY NO ONE FINDS OUT!

HAH! NAILED IT!

"PIKKIBALL, GO!"

WHERE AM I?

AHH!! PIKKIBALL, GO!

OW! HEY!

DANY?

HELLO, ME.

GAH! SORRY! I FREAKED OUT.

LET ME EXPLAIN.

I THINK I GET IT! I'M LIKE, YOUR LIFE DISASTER CONSULTANT. CLONE EDITION.

SO THIS IS WHAT I LOOK LIKE TO EVERYONE? AND SOUND LIKE? MY VOICE SOUNDS SO WEIRD.

I KNOW, RIGHT?

39

40

OOH!!

THESE ARE ALL THE BOOKS **MOM** SAID I CAN'T READ...

BANNED

GIRD YOUR **LOINS!** Lurid descriptions of the female Victorian ankle shocked Victorian audiences when book was banned

WOW!

AWESOME, RIGHT? MAKE YOURSELF AT HOME.

WUH-WHAT IS **THIS?!**

YOU KNOW WHAT IT IS.

NO ONE CAN KNOW OF MY CRUSH!!!! I WILL GO TO THE **GRAVE** WITH THIS SECRET!!! IT'S TOO EMBARRASSING!!!

FLOPP

I KNOW. I'LL JUST **DIE** IF ANYONE FINDS OUT.

HE'S SO CUTE. LOOK AT THIS ONE—

IT'S HIS HAIR. HE HAS COOL HAIR.

yeah...

HE LOVES SCI-FI **AND** POETRY...

HE'S ALSO **NICE**...

You can copy my homework

yay!

I BET HE'S REALLY DEEP. I CAN JUST TELL.

TOTALLY! HE SAID SOMETHING THIS MORNING— UH—

Memory.exe

· Pinecone

"[LAZINESS IS] THE ROOT OF HUMAN INNOVATION."

SO DEEP!

HE'S NOT THE CLASSICAL, GET-GOOD-GRADES TYPE... MORE OF A...

CLON LABS

MISUNDERSTOOD GENIUS. JUST LIKE US. HEHEHE.

HE WOULDN'T SPELL "SWEET" WRONG, WOULD HE?

M-MAYBE HIS HAND SLIPPED WHEN HE WAS WRITING.

YEAH.

ELCOME

ICE

WOW... YOU HAVE A FOOD FOUNTAIN...

I ALSO HAVE CRIME STREETS 3.

LET'S SEE WHO'S A BETTER STREET CRIMINAL!

CLONE VS. Dany classic

3 HOURS LATER

WOW, YOU'RE REALLY GOOD AT **CRIME STREETS**!

BUT, CLONEY, YOU TOTALLY CREAMED ME!

I GUESS I'M... REALLY **REALLY** GOOD.

CLONES RULE!

I got BLISTERS on me fingers!!

OW!!

ha ha we're hilarious ♡

YOU KNOW, I DON'T KNOW WHAT'S WRONG WITH CARA. I'M SO MUCH FUN TO HANG OUT WITH!

braiding our hair together →

YAY

ha ha

FUN

LoL

ME TOO! I AGREE! HAHAHA!

YOU **WOULD** AGREE, WOULDN'T YOU, CLONEY!

44

OH YEAH. WE'RE DEFINITELY ON THE SAME PAGE. HOW ABOUT YOU CHILL OUT HERE AND I'LL DO YOUR HOMEWORK AS A LITTLE THANK-YOU FOR BRINGING ME INTO THIS WORLD.

Sounds like a plan!

THIS WAS A QUESTIONABLE DECISION.

wah

VR WORKOUT
HAMSTER WHEEL EDITION

IMAGINE YOU'RE NOT EXERCISING!

LVL 1: CENTAURED + BALANCED

WELCOME

SINK

COULD YOU HELP ME WITH SOME—

OH, DANY, YOU'RE ACTUALLY DOING YOUR HOMEWORK! I'M SO PROUD OF YOU!

Um, mom? Do you know how to FOIL?

Uh—

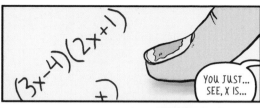

You just... see, X is...

Why don't you ever ask me for help with the FUN stuff, like your English homework?

That's cuz it's easy!

Ask your sister!

I'm going out with my FRIENDS. My math notes from seventh grade are in the basement, though.

Nah.

Ugh, I give up!

Booooo!

C'mon, Dany, you can do it!

Well, I tried.

I CAN'T HAVE *THREE* OF US RUNNING AROUND!

MAYBE YOU SHOULD MAKE ANOTHER CLONE. LIKE, A REALLY *SCHOLARLY* ONE.

...*SHE'D* PROBABLY BE LAZY, *TOO!*

YOU READY FOR YOUR FIRST DAY OF SCHOOL?

I GUESS SO! TIME TO TAKE THE WORLD BY STORM!

hug

MY DAUGHTER... THEY GROW UP SO FAST.

you got this

OKAY, I'LL BE IN THE PIKKIBALL IF YOU NEED ME.

YAWN

grumble

CLÖN LABS

EGGS

You selected

scrambled eggs

PUSH

funny side up
scrambled
hard boiled
french toast

what's the answer to this?

DANIELLE?

ROBBER BARONS!!

That's not what I was looking for, but actually a fascinating response—

snort

HISTORY

I COULD STAY IN HERE AND NEVER LEAVE.

CLÖN LABS

YOU SURE ABOUT THAT? I MIGHT GO ROGUE AND TAKE OVER YOUR LIFE FOREVER.

HAH! GO FOR IT.

DANY, I'M THIRSTY. BE A *PAL* AND GO GET ME A *DIET LEMON CHELTZER*.

?

WHY ME?

LOOK, IF YOU REALLY WANNA BE *COOL*...

It's a test!

...YOU'LL GET ME A CHELTZER.

GET THE CHELTZER!

WHAT IF I GET YOU ONE IN THE CAF? MADISON AND ALEESHA ARE ABANDONING US.

UGH. *FINE.*

49

WAIT UP!

Hahaha Wait really? Yeah, F=M v

WHERE'D YOU GO? APPARENTLY I BOMBED THE POP QUIZ TOO. TWINSIES!

yay?

IT'S NOT *OUR* FAULT! I MEAN, WHO GIVES A POP QUIZ ON A WEDNESDAY?!

UM. THE WHOLE *POINT* OF POP QUIZZES IS THEY CAN HAPPEN AT ANY TIME.

IT JUST FEELS CRUEL! IT'S LIKE, THE *FURTHEST* DAY FROM THE WEEKEND, IF YOU THINK ABOUT IT...

ON, LIKE, EITHER SIDE OF THE... CALENDAR...

OH, DANY, WHAT ARE YOU BLABBERING ABOUT? SO CRINGEY! MY VOICE IS SO ANNOYING!

HOW DO I CHANGE THE *CHANNEL* ON THIS THING?! STOP TALKING! *ABORT!!*

DID YOU JUST WHISPER "ABORT" IN A TINY VOICE?

UM. N-NO...

ACK! HOW CAN I RUIN THINGS FROM *INSIDE* THE PIKKIBALL?! I'M SORRY, CLONEY!

Sighhh...

SPORT 1 TEAM

guh...

...SO BY THAT POINT, HE'S COMPLETELY UNDERWATER, BUT HE JUST KEEPS—

...ANYWAY, IT WAS PRETTY HILARIOUS AT THE TIME.

ha ha me

DID SOMEONE ORDER A CHELTZER?

...I THOUGHT THE QUIZ WAS *EASY*.

PTHHT!

SO EASY, I DID IT IN MY SLEEP!

I *SAW* THAT!

...I SLEPT THROUGH THE QUIZ!

DANY! THAT'S TERRIBLE!

ha ha

IS THAT SOMETHING YOU'RE *PROUD* OF?

WHAT A FOOL I WAS!

I'm... annoying.

52

OH MY GOD, SHUUUT UP!

...WHAT? I HAVE SENSITIVE EARS.

guh...

TOSS!

YA BLEW IT!

I THOUGHT YOU GUYS MADE UP.

WE DID, WE DID.

WHERE ARE YOU GOING? COME BACK.

BACK AWAY

I DON'T WANT TO FEEL LIKE I'M TALKING ON EGGSHELLS, SO—

WHAT ARE YOU TALKING ABOUT?

yeah

Dany?

OCO

CHOCO

IT'S A PLAY ON WORDS! PEACE OUT!

fury & loathing

mild sympathy

NONONO! TURN BACK AND GROVEL!

YOU CAN'T TALK TO CARA LIKE THAT! SHE'LL DESTROY US!

I DIDN'T DO IT EITHER...

IF YA KNOW WHAT I MEAN.

WINK★

ALERT!! WINK ACTIVATED

OH MY GOD, YOU DID NOT JUST **WINK!!!**

OH, GOOD, THAT MEANS THE ANSWERS WILL ACTUALLY BE RIGHT THIS TIME!

ha ha

...TROUBLE AT THE GIRL TABLE AGAIN?

YEAH. CARA MCCOY TOTALLY HATES ME.

shrug

WHAT HAPPENED?

SHE SEEMS TO HAVE AN ISSUE WITH MY...

LOUD VOICE...

AMONG OTHER THINGS...

YOU'RE NOT SO BAD. THE **CAFETERIA** IS LOUD. VOLUME IS RELATIVE.

YOU'RE JUST **BOISTEROUS**.

...THINK IT HAS SOMETHING TO DO WITH MADISON?

IF ONLY CARA KNEW THE... SPECIAL CIRCUMSTANCES... OF MY FRIENDSHIP WITH MADISON...

I DUNNO. MAYBE.

THAT SHOULD PROBABLY BE MADISON'S CALL, THOUGH, RIGHT?

YEAH.

WASH YOUR LUNCH

HERE'S THE THING: I LITERALLY **PAID** CARA TO PRETEND TO BE MY FRIEND, SO I FEEL OWED JUST A **SLIVER** OF RESPECT FROM HER.

ha ha

lame...

IF NOT **REAL** RESPECT, THEN **PRETEND** RESPECT AT LEAST.

heh heh

YOU SHOULD SEE IF YOU CAN GET A REFUND. THAT'S **BREACH OF CONTRACT.**

DANY! YOU'RE AIRING OUR DIRTY LAUNDRY...

DID YOU HEAR PRINCIPAL FLINSKY IS RETIRING? HE GOT SOME HUGE INHERITANCE.

wHAT?!!

SLAM

HE'S MOVING TO A RANCH IN ARIZONA.

YOU ARE loud...

THAT'S NOT RIGHT! **RETIREMENT?!** THE MAN IS, WHAT, FORTY-FIVE?!

HE SHOULD USE HIS "INHERITANCE" TO PAY FOR THE **GYM REPAIRS.**

WHY WOULD HE—

OHHH.

WAIT, WHY WOULD HE PAY FOR GYM REPAIRS OUT OF HIS OWN PERSONAL FUNDS?

WHAT AM I MISSING HERE? ARE YOU HINTING AT SOMETH—

NOTHING.

IT'S JUST FOR THE GREATER GOOD?! HE DIDN'T EARN THAT MONEY. IT JUST FELL IN HIS LAP.

YEAH. IT'S LIKE SPIDERBAT SAYS: "WITH GREAT WEALTH COMES A LOT OF RESPONSIBILITY."

YOU GUYS ARE CRAZY.

Yeah!

SPIDERBAT'S LIFE LESSONS ASIDE, PRINCIPAL FLINSKY CAN DO WHATEVER HE WANTS WITH HIS MONEY AS LONG AS WE LIVE IN A CAPITALIST SOCIETY.

BRRINGGG

boo capitalism!

see ya, bud

bye

I FEEL LIKE **WE** HAVE RESPONSIBILITIES TOO.

r-responsibility??

LIKE, WHY ELSE WOULD WE HAVE THESE AMAZING POWERS?

58

OH! YEAH. THAT COULD BE FUN. WE SHOULD...

...WE SHOULD, LIKE, PRACTICE OUR SOLAR POWERS™ AND SCOUT FOR VILLAINY TOGETHER SOMETIME.

YOU **WHAT?!** AHH!!!!

ACK!

THAT'D BE RAD!!!

WHAT?

PLUS ULTRA!

ha ha

hey watch it !!!!!

SINK !!

PHEW. HOMEWORK TIME. **I CAN DO THIS.**

REALLY I'LOVE MY FAMILY

7th Grade

7th Grade

LAUREN'S MATH NOTES! NICE!

SUDS of ANARCHY
LAUNDRY DETERGENT

ROMANO. MATH
7th GR. L. RADLEY

MATH

60

JACKPOT!!

LAUREN, YOU SAVED EVERY TEST?! I LOVE YOU?!

SUDS of ANARCHY

hup!

noooooo

CRASH

UGH! DANG IT!

THE DOOR!

SALAMI?

Sniff

UH... WHAT DID I JUST DO?!

I *DUNNO*, CLONEY.

CLÖN LABS

STIR

SHADY MEN? I GUESS IT **IS** AN EMERGENCY.

THEY'LL FIX THE SALAMI DOOR.

WE SHOULD SEND ONE TO LOOK FOR THE BLUE DOG!

YEAH!

SEEK YE THE DOG WITH PELT OF BLUE.

WHO'D HAVE THOUGHT WE'D EVEN **NEED** AN ARMY OF TEMPORARY MUD-BASED AUTOMATONS?

OH NO, THE FIRE DEPARTMENT IS HERE...

WEEOO WEEOO WEEOO

EVERYONE SAW ME! THEY ALL KNOW MY SECRET... WHAT DO I DO?

THE TRUTH WILL SET YOU FREE.

NOT IN THIS SCENARIO! NOT IF THEY TELL THE **GROWN-UPS** THAT I HAVE **MAGIC!**

DETRANSFORM, LEAH! DON'T LET THEM SEE YOU LIKE THAT!

WHY DON'T WE JUST TURN BACK TIME OR SOMETHING?

GEE, MADISON, THAT'S A BIT DRASTIC?

I'VE GOT IT! WE CAN...

WE CAN JUST WIPE EVERYONE'S MINDS.

JUST OF THE GYM BATTLE. SOFTEN THEIR MEMORIES WITH SOME ENCHANTED FREE T-SHIRTS.

NO ONE CAN RESIST FREE T-SHIRTS!

SKRATCH

POOF

...AND WE CAN HAVE THESE **MUD CREATURES** HAND OUT THE SHIRTS!!

MUD...?

Bag 'o Shirts

WHAT DO YOU THINK THAT BLUE DOG WAS? WHY WAS IT IN A BOTTLE?

WHAT WOULD OUR PARENTS WANT WITH **BOTTLED DOG?**

DO YOU THINK THEY KNOW ABOUT... MAGIC?

I DESPERATELY DON'T **WANT** THEM TO, BUT... SIGNS POINT TO... **SOMETHING.**

MAYBE WE SHOULD SPLIT UP AND LOOK FOR THIS DOG?

Good idea...

SIGH...

69

...OOH, WHAT IF YOUR **DAD** CHAPERONES THE SCHOOL DANCE. WHEN'S HE BACK FROM NEW YORK?

I DON'T KNOW.

HE'S GOT AN APARTMENT IN MIDTOWN. HIS OFFICE NEEDS HIM ALL THE TIME.

NOT THAT **MOM** EVEN CARES.

...WOULD YOU COME WITH ME?

MAYBE YOU CAN VISIT HIM, HAVE A FUN DAY IN THE CITY TOGETHER.

SURE.

70

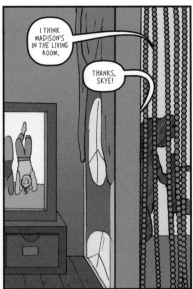

I THINK MADISON'S IN THE LIVING ROOM.

THANKS, SKYE!

MADISON! LEVEL 100 EMERGENCY!

BURST

FLAIL

WHA-?!

THUNK

Breathe into your spine...

OH, UH, NEVER MIND.

HHHI, CARA.

WHAT HAPPENED?!

OH, UH, LEVEL 100 IS THE LOWEST LEVEL. LEVEL 1 IS THE HIGHEST LEVEL. IT'S, UH, THE METRIC SYSTEM.

TELL ME.

CARA? I'VE GOTTA HELP DANY WITH A THING.

FINE, I'LL SEE YOU LATER.

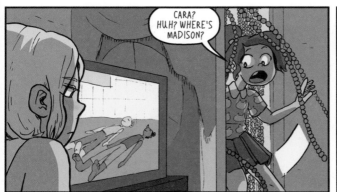

WHAT IS THE FUNCTION OF A BLUE DOG IN A BOTTLE?

BEATS ME. DAD ALWAYS SAYS NO DOGS ALLOWED.

...WHICH IS JUST *SO* HYPOCRITICAL NOW.

BUT HE DOESN'T EVEN *LIKE* DOGS, SO IT DOESN'T REALLY ADD UP...

WOL·MORT

WHERE DO YOU THINK THEY GOT IT?

IT MUST HAVE COME FROM GREAT-AUNT ELMA'S ESTATE. I MEAN, THAT'S WHERE I GOT MY MAGIC *SKETCHBOOK*...

GIMME

...AND THIS DOG SOMEHOW TURNED THE BACK DOOR INTO *SALAMI!*

WANT SOME?

SKYE AND REX ARE PESCATARIANS.

I'M SO SORRY.

MMM, THIS IS GOOD SALAMI.

EVER PUT SALAMI IN THE MICROWAVE? IT'S REALLY GOOD.

OH?

OH MY GOD... UNRELATED, BUT DIDN'T YOUR PARENTS JUST WIN THE *CASH4LYFE LOTTO?*

74

YEAH...

AND YOUR MOM, SHE LOST A TON OF WEIGHT--

SHE WENT ON, LIKE...

...A CRASH DIET... IT WAS REALLY SUDDEN...

DOG GENIE!!

THEY WOULDN'T...

NO?

OH MY GOD. DOG GENIE.

whistle

...YOUR **MOTHER** LETS YOU DYE YOUR HAIR PINK?

I'M AN **ORPHAN!**

MELTON ANIMAL CONTROL

THE ANIMAL SHELTER WAS PRETTY PSYCHED ABOUT THAT $2 MILLION DONATION FROM OUR "ECCENTRIC GREAT-AUNT."

HAH. NICE COVER STORY. I BET THEY THINK WE'RE IN THE MOB.

...GUH, **I** NEED A COVER STORY! WHAT LIE DO I TELL MY PARENTS IF—

DOG PARK

MAYBE WE CAN EXPLAIN IT TO THEM. YOUR PARENTS ARE PRETTY CHILL.

NOT REALLY. THEY'RE ALWAYS MAD AT ME AND TELLING ME WHAT TO DO.

DOG PARK

REX AND SKYE WOULD **NEVER** TELL ME WHAT TO DO.

THAT'S COOL.

NAH, IT'S JUST AWKWARD.

76

IT'S LIKE... WE ALL KNOW THEY'RE NOT MY PARENTS, NOT REALLY.

SO THEY CAN'T YELL AT ME, IT'S LIKE I'M A HOUSEGUEST.

BUT I CAN'T ACT OUT--

HEY!

CHOMP

That's him!!

CONTROL YOUR STUPID DOG!

SPRINT

STAY!!

FWOO

I wish I had REAL PARENTS!

BRUFF!

You are not my master.

BING BING BING

♥♥♥♥♥ 6:03

Mama Bear
yesterday
Do we have potatoes?

Yeah

Thanks

Now
WHERE R U??
OMG
COME HOME NOW!!

...

FWOOF

Sparkly...

78

DANIELLE!

WARP

WHAT DID YOU DO?!?!

Y-YOU DON'T NEED TO WITNESS THIS.

SQUEEZE

GET IN HERE!

WHY ARE YOU HERE, MADISON?

hey Linda

SO YOUR MAGIC DOG GENIE RAN AWAY. LOOKS LIKE YOUR WISHES STUCK AROUND, THOUGH.

MADISON!

YOU KNOW ABOUT MAGIC?! ABOUT THE HINN?!

79

OH, I **KNOW** ABOUT MAGIC.

ahem

I KNOCKED OVER THE LAMP AND THE DOG CAME OUT.

PUSH AWAY

WELL, WHERE DID IT GO?

IT RAN AWAY! MADISON AND I WERE TRYING TO CATCH IT!

I— I THOUGHT WE REALLY COVERED OUR TRACKS—

YOU LEFT THE **BROKEN SHARDS** OF OUR **MAGIC GENIE LAMP** IN THE **DRIVEWAY**, DANY! IT WAS THE FIRST THING I SAW WHEN I CAME HOME!

WHOOPS.

WHO KNOWS **WHAT** THE HINN WILL DO ON ITS OWN—

YOU NEED TO RESPECT OUR BELONGINGS—

YELL YELL YELL YELL YELL YELL YELL

80

DID YOU WISH TO BE SKINNY, MOM?

...

LINDA! OF ALL THE THINGS TO WISH FOR!

LOOK, MADISON, WHEN *YOU'VE* WALKED A MILE IN MY SHOES—

LINDA DOESN'T HAVE TO EXPLAIN HERSELF TO YOU!

AND *YOU* WISHED FOR A GUITAR AND A LUCKY LOTTO TICKET?

GUITAR—? I STARTED PLAYING FOR STRESS MANAGEMENT. AND THAT LOTTO TICKET IS *PROVIDING* FOR—

HONEY, REMIND ME TO CALL THE COMPANY, THERE'S SOMETHING WRONG WITH THE PAPERWORK *AGAIN*—

DANIELLE RADLEY, YOU ARE GROUNDED.

GIVE ME YOUR LAPTOP— YOUR PHONE—

I WANT YOU COMING STRAIGHT HOME FROM SCHOOL—

NO FUN—!!

WHAAT?! FOR HOW LONG?

A MONTH!

CAN'T I KEEP MY PHONE FOR EMERGENCIES?

nod ((

OKAY, BUT YOU REALLY ARE GROUNDED, YOU KNOW.

FINE! HERE'S MY MAGIC REMOTE CONTROL AND MYSTICAL INSECT REPELLANT RING.

THAT'S ALL THE MAGIC I HAVE.

REALLY?

I SWEAR ON THE HOLY BIBLE.

...I DIDN'T TAKE ANYTHING FROM ELMA'S, REMEMBER?

GOOD. THANK YOU, SWEETIE. I DON'T WANT YOU MESSING AROUND WITH MAGIC AND GETTING HURT.

BUT WE ARE GOING TO HAVE TO TALK ABOUT THIS.

A LOT.

nooooooooo

WHO'S GOING TO CATCH THE DOG, THEN?

WHAT?

I WAS JUST WONDERING WHO WAS GOING TO CATCH THE *DOG* IF *DANY* CAN'T LEAVE THE HOUSE.

ARE *YOU* TELLING *ME* WHAT TO DO?!

shhh

DO YOU THINK ANIMAL CONTROL CAN HANDLE A *GENIE*?

AND EVEN IF SOMEHOW THEY *COULD*— COULDN'T THEY TRACE THIS *HINN* BACK TO *YOU*?

YOU'RE RIGHT. DANY, *YOU* LOST THE DOG, *YOU* HAVE TO FIND IT.

I UNDERSTAND.

YOU'RE STILL *EXTREMELY* GROUNDED! GO TO YOUR ROOM! WE'RE GONNA TALK LATER. I'M *VERY* DISAPPOINTED.

MADISON, HONEY, YOU NEED A RIDE HOME?

OKAY!

TRUDGE

SIGHHHH...

...WHERE'S CLONEY?

...NICE AND **CONVENIENT** THAT SHE **MISSED** THIS WHOLE DISASTROUS SCENE.

MOTO PSYCHO
SUMMER
CUPS
CINEMA

POXAR
presents
CUPS

Ding!

GOOD GRADES

Be Best

Ding!

A SUPER Family

6:13

MADISON:
We have a dog genie on the loose
Meet in the woods at 7 to discuss

LEAH:
WHaT?????
also im supposed to have
dinner with my family?

TOM:
!!!!

...Double Dany...?

...Here she is now!!

tee hee

smirk

Pikki...?

I TELL YOU, THIS IS HOW PEOPLE SHOULD LIVE.

hm...

IN A LITTLE PIKKIBALL? SEEMS A BIT LONELY.

WHIRRR

whinny!

Chef Penny Sez:
Enjoy Your
'SPAGHETTI'

IT'S FINE!
EVERYTHING'S
FINE!

CHECK **THIS**
OUT!

spaghetti?

Why did
you—?

ew.

SINK

NO
RULES!

WHERE
DOES
IT GO?

I dunno!

I CAN'T EVEN MESS UP THIS PLACE
IF I TRY. IT'S LIKE I TYPED IN
THE CHEAT CODE OF LIFE.
MY **ROSEBUD**.

FLOP

I USED THE CHEAT CODE OF LIFE
IN **THE SINS: HOUSE PARTY** AND
IT MADE THE WHOLE GAME
POINTLESS.

88

SHE'S HOW MY SOLAR POWER MANIFESTED! HER NAME IS BUDJAWUDJA. I TAUGHT HER TO SHRINK.

...BUDJAWUDJA?

KISS

IT'S BECAUSE SHE'S A *CUTE WITTLE BUDJAWUDJA!!*

BUDJAWUDJA, SHRINK!

BEEM

AWW!

snif

HEHE, THAT TICKLES!

CAN'T BELIEVE YOU SNUCK OUT THE NIGHT YOUR PARENTS GROUNDED YOU!

IT WAS MADISON'S IDEA!!

Shameless!

HEY, *DANY SQUARED* LOST A DOG GENIE, AND I THOUGHT IT SOUNDED LIKE A JOB FOR THE SOLAR GEEKS.

WOO! A SOLAR MISSION!

THE LONGER THE DOG GENIE IS LOOSE, THE MORE DANGER EVERYONE IN MELTON IS IN!

WE CAN SET UP PATROLS, DO RESEARCH ON—

HEY! LOOK!

"*HINN*. THE ETERNAL COMPANION AND SERVANT TO AN UPPER ECHELON OF DEITIES, THIS TYPE OF DJINN APPEARS AS A FAITHFUL DOG."

HIST OF MAG

Dieties PLURAL??

DOOM DOOM

ALERT: LIN A

MOM!!

NO! GUH! INITIALIZE CONTROLS!

eject

INT. BEDROOM

WE MADE A HOLOGRAM THAT PRETENDS TO DO HOMEWORK.

...IT WAS HER IDEA.

HONEY?

h-hi, Mom!

H-HI, MOM! JUST DOING MY HOMEWORK.

SORRY TO INTERRUPT.

YOU KNOW, I CAN'T HELP FEELING LIKE A HYPOCRITE.

THERE I AM, YELLING AT YOU FOR PLAYING WITH A *MAGIC REMOTE CONTROL* AND A *CITRONELLA RING*, WHEN I'VE DONE SO MUCH WORSE.

I DIDN'T KNOW— WHEN I RUBBED THAT MAGIC LAMP—

I MEAN, I RUBBED IT WITH A *LYSOIL WIPE*. I DIDN'T KNOW IT WAS *MAGIC*. I DIDN'T UNDERSTAND THE CONSEQUENCES.

...THAT DOG IS NOT GOOD AT GRANTING WISHES.

DANIELLE, HONEY, I DON'T WANT YOU FALLING INTO THE SAME TRAP. YOU HAVE TO BE BETTER THAN ME.

WH-WHAT'S WRONG WITH YOUR WISH?

ha
ha

I DIDN'T.

REACH

FLINCH!

hurt

HIRY
OTTER

...

SORRY.
SOMEDAY YOU'LL
UNDERSTAND.

YOU LIE TO YOUR PARENTS **SO EASILY...**

Mom...

I THINK I REALLY HURT MY MOM'S FEELINGS.

Aww... Cloney...

LINDA'S TOUGH, SHE CAN HANDLE IT.

SHE—

SHE WOULD'VE PUT HER HAND THROUGH THE HOLOGRAM... IF I DIDN'T...

:SIGH:

copying to "Mom"

MOM

exit

PLAN.doc

PATROLS:
✦Cloney & Dany daily✦
① Joan & Leah
     (Mon.)
② Madison &
     Aleesha (wed)
③ Dany (Cloney?)
     & Tom (Thur.)

31

HAND MY PARENTS THESE MEMORY-SOFTENING T-SHIRTS. THEY SHOULD MAKE ME UNGROUNDED.

AND UNHURT MOM'S FEELINGS.

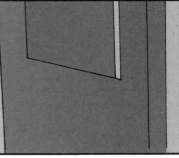

WELCOME HOME, SWEETHEART.

I THOUGHT YOU WERE IN YOUR ROOM.

I ♥ MY DAUGHTER

THE FAULT IN OUR KIDS by JUAN VERDE

I, UH... HUH?

blink blink

YOU'RE SUPPOSED TO BE **GROUNDED**!

WHY? DANY'S BEEN SO GOOD!

I ♥ my daughter

CHUCK? ARE YOU—

I LOVE MY DAUGHTER.

I ♥ my daughter

DANY! WHAT DID YOU DO?!!

HOW DID YOU EVEN DO THIS?!

DID YOU—

DID YOU CATCH THE HINN?

N-NO... I...

I USED MAGIC!!!

PARENTAL DISAPPOINTMENT

...I CAN'T BELIEVE YOU'D BE SO DECEITFUL!

YOU LIED TO MY FACE!

AND IF I HADN'T BEEN WEARING MY PROTECTION AMULET—

WHAT DID SHE DO?

no no nooOoOoo wake up Dany

I DON'T KNOW, CHUCK, SOME SORT OF SPELL?

MOM, I— I'M SORRY—

99

YOU'RE SORRY YOU GOT **CAUGHT**.

DOESN'T THAT COUNT?

HOW DID I **BELIEVE** YOU WHEN YOU SAID THAT WAS ALL THE MAGIC YOU HAD?

OH MY GOD! IT WAS RIGHT THERE IN FRONT OF US—

THE GRAPHIC MEMOIR, CHUCK!

H-HOW DO YOU KNOW ABOUT—

I FOUND IT IN YOUR WASTEBASKET. IT WAS JUST SITTING THERE!

DAD AND I THOUGHT IT WAS CUTE. I WAS SO PROUD OF YOUR CREATIVITY.

SO OUTLANDISH, I NEVER EVEN THOUGHT IT COULD BE TRUE.

WHEN REALLY, IT WAS A CONFESSION.

—!

STOMP STOMP STOMP

POOR MADISON... SO SHE'S YOUR...

...IMAGINARY FRIEND...?

FLIP

She's a real person!! (did you even read it?!)

...WHERE IS IT?

FLIP
FLIP

...THE SKETCHBOOK?

SPRINT!

SLAM

yell
yell

MOM... PLEASE... DON'T USE THE SKETCHBOOK.

I WON'T. I PROMISE.

OKAY.

...

HOW CAN I TRUST YOU AGAIN?

BZZT!

I THOUGHT SHE'D **NEVER** SHUT UP.

snif...

I'VE LEARNED MY LESSON.

GET REALLY, REALLY GOOD AT HIDING OUR TRACKS.

I MEAN, DOES SHE REALLY EXPECT US TO **LISTEN** TO HER? SO NAIVE.

AN EXACT REPLICA OF MY MAGIC SKETCHBOOK, WITH THE MAGIC INTACT.

IN YOUR **FACE**, MOM!

RUMBLE RUMBLE

"DOOM"

KRrrr

WUH-WHAT DID WE DO?!

LIMITLESS ROLL OF UNIVERSAL REPAIR TAPE! *PLEASE* TELL ME THIS NEW SKETCHBOOK WORKS!

KRRRR

IT'S-- IT'S NOT WORKING--

shake shake

KRRR

105

IT'S WORKING!

...HEAR SOMETHING, CHUCK?

YEAH.

Guh...

DID YOU HEAR THAT?!

HEAR WHAT?

I HEARD A LOUD SOUND— I *FELT* IT.

...I DUNNO. MAYBE THE CIACCIOS' TREE FINALLY FELL.

badump badump

OH.

YOU KNOW THAT IT'S WRONG TO MIND-CONTROL, DON'T YOU, DANY?

YEAH.

IT SCARES ME THAT YOU'D EVEN TRY.

⌐I'M SORRY.

I NEED TO BE ABLE TO TRUST YOU.

YOU LOOK SO GREAT, LINDA.

C'MERE, ADELE.

UNHH! I LOVE IT WHEN MOM COOKS! REMINDS ME OF THE GOOD OLD DAYS.

REMEMBER HOW MOM USED TO MAKE THAT MAYO SALMON CASSEROLE, EVERY YEAR ON MY BIRTHDAY? SHE SAYS SHE'LL—

HA! GOOD DAYS. WITH DAD?

YOU EXAGGERATE, DAVE. DAD'S JUST STRICT. AND—

—AND KEEP IT DOWN. *SOME* OF US DON'T BURN EVERY BRIDGE WE CROSS.

YEAH, DAVE. YOU DON'T GET TO CHOOSE FAMILY.

HMPH.

I'M GOOD. LOOKS DELICIOUS, THOUGH.

IT *IS* DELICIOUS! *I* MADE IT!

YOU HARDLY ATE, LINDA! AT LEAST HAVE SOME PIE?

YOU LOOK GREAT ALREADY, LINDA. YOU DON'T WANT TO TAKE YOUR DIET TOO FAR...

IN A BIT, TRACY.

DID I TELL YOU— CHARLIE WON'T EAT CAKE ANYMORE! HE DOESN'T LIKE IT! CAN YOU BELIEVE IT?

WHAT AN ADVANCED PALATE, RIGHT?

SUSAN AND I JUST GOT A CALL FROM MRS. CORMANSKI. SHE SAYS **CHARLIE** MIGHT HAVE TO **SKIP** A GRADE OR TWO.

WOW.

THEY FINALLY NOTICED—

—WHAT A SMART ONE THIS IS. CHIP OFF THE OLD BLOCK.

PAT PAT

...He doesn't love me.

SQUIRM

OH, DAVE, CONGRATS ON THE BREAKTHROUGH. SUSAN WAS JUST TELLING ME—

THEY'VE NEVER SEEN ANYTHING LIKE IT. WE'VE GOT GOVERNMENT CONTRACTORS SNIFFING AROUND MY WORK AT THE LAB.

slide

...SO THEY **FINALLY** OFFERED ME TENURE. MASTERSON TOLD ME THEY **WOULDN'T**, BUT HE'S EATING HIS WORDS NOW.

NARESZCIE. BETTER LATE THAN NEVER.

I NEVER HEAR OF A PROFESSOR GETTING **TENURE** AFTER SO LONG DEFERRED—

IT'S NOT THAT UNCOMMON! YOU DON'T KNOW WHAT YOU'RE TALKING ABOUT, **DAD.**

111

...WHOLE FAMILY OF *LOST CAUSES.*

Thanks, Grandpa...

SEEMS LIKE WE'RE ALL FINALLY FIGURING THINGS OUT.

DAVE WITH THE LAB...

LINDA WITH YOUR DIET, AND CHUCK WITH HIS *CASH4LYFE,* AND ME WITH THIS RECORD REAL ESTATE BOOM!

(YOU CAN BENEFIT FROM THE BOOM TOO, IF YOU WANT MY HELP!)

CASH TODAY!

FREE APPRAISAL!

10%

CALL AUNT TRACY NOW!!! (203) 555-1789

IT'S AS IF THINGS ARE *FINALLY* COMING TOGETHER FOR ALL OF US. THE WAY IT'S ALWAYS MEANT TO HAVE BEEN.

CHEERS TO THAT!

CLINK

CLINK

heh

WHAT'S SO FUNNY, TRACE?

NOTHING, NOTHING. After you...

CAN I OFFER YOU A SODA, DANIELLE?

ER... SURE.

YOU WANNA GOODIE?

DO YOU LOVE CHEESE?

YIP!

YOU DO!

CHOMP CHOMP

BabyTab™

NEWS LOCAL MU

KILLER CLOWN STILL ON THE LOOSE, UNREPENTANT—

vandalized. Could it be the Blue Bandit?

School emergency funding falls through

PURP BOY

...al store vandalized: Could it be the **BLUE BANDIT?**

Blue Bandit Fan concept art

Dusty's Old-Fashioned Vacuum Warehouse was vandalized last night, its entire inventory of vacuum cleaners destroyed beyond repair. ...a mysterious blur locals have ...bed The Blue Bandit, captured ...curity footage, is the only lead ...estigators so far.

YOU'VE NOTICED IT TOO? SOMETHING'S NOT RIGHT IN **MELTON.**

huh?

JUMP

Is BabyTab spying on your child? Yes.

MISSING PERSONS REPORTS SPIKE IN MELTON, CT
was it something I said?

weath

MELTON PET STORE ROBBED
REGISTER UNTOUCHED

You've reached your free article limit. SUBSCRIBE?

Owner...

BLUEBANDITWATCH .COM

BLUE BANDIT: **URBAN LEGEND** OR **PUBLIC MENACE?**

POLL:
◉ urban legend
◉ menace

Evidence? Blue Bandit T-shi...

SCROLL SCROLL

BabyTab™

BLUE BANDIT
MELT...

VACUUM WAREHOUSE VANDALIZED
DUSTY OLD-FASH...
VACU... WAR...
BLUE BAND... SUSP...

Dusty's OLD FASHIONED **VACUUM WAREHOUS...**

11:40

WANTED
BLUE BANDIT

NO DUMPLING...

cuuute...

you're gonna get rabies

nuk?

114

LOCAL NEWS
SPEEDING TICKET ISSUED
TOP 10 BLUE BANDIT FAN THEORIES "..."

FOR YO
why don'
have frie

SHOVE

NICK MALONEY! THAT'S **MY** LOCKER! WHAT ARE YOU DOING?!

NOTH—

YOU'VE BEEN LEAVING ME THOSE **SECRET ADMIRER NOTES?!**

I **SAVED** YOU! YOU WERE A **PIG!** AND THIS—

A PIG?

DO YOU REALLY NEED TO RUIN MY LIFE?! WHY NOT TAKE A DAY OFF?

HUH?

NICK LIKES THAT GIRL?

?

HAH! SHE THOUGHT I **ACTUALLY** HAD A **CRUSH** ON HER.

Oh

BUT IT WAS ALL JUST A PRANK.

...harsh

WHY WOULD YOU MESS WITH SOMEONE'S HEAD LIKE THAT?

YOU'RE AN EASY TARGET.

OMG DRAMAAA

OOOOHHH

OOOHHHH

FIGHT! FIGHT!

CHOC

I CAN DESTROY YOU A THOUSAND DIFFERENT WAYS. BUT I WON'T.

ohhh!!

...I SHOULD'VE **KNOWN** IT WAS YOU WHEN I SAW THE **AWFUL SPELLING** AND **CLICHÉD IMAGERY**.

Ohhh

CLONEY!

ARE YOU OKAY?

I SOLVED THE MYSTERY OF THE SECRET ADMIRER NOTES. IT WAS...

NICK MALONEY.

AW, HONEY...

Shut.

CHOCO...

YOU WANT ME TO BEAT HIM UP FOR YOU?

SIGH. NAH.

I'M **SO** READY FOR **REAL DANY** TO GET CABIN FEVER IN HER PIKKIBALL AND DECIDE TO LIVE HER OWN LIFE.

HINT, HINT.

UHH, I'M GOOD...

(SOME THOUGHTS ON WIGGING OUT IN THE HALLWAY, THOUGH...)

SUP Real Dany

HEY, CAN I BORROW YOUR *FLYING RING* FOR A FEW DAYS?

YOU LOSE YOURS?

I'M ALWAYS LOSING MINE; I HAVE LIKE THREE AT HOME.

KEEP IT!

HEY, GUYS.

YESTERDAY WAS MADISON'S AND MY DAY TO PATROL FOR THE HINN—

THE BLUE BANDIT!

IT DOES SEEM PRETTY LIKELY THEY'RE ONE AND THE SAME.

I WANTED TO SEE THE PUPPY AGAIN...

YEAH, THERE WAS NOTHING GOING ON.

AND I WAS THINKING... THE HINN MIGHT NOT *WANT* US TO FIND IT.

IF WE COULD ONLY *MAKE* IT WANT... OOH, RICE CRUNCHIES!

...ALEESHA STILL WANTED US TO "HELP THE WORLD" OR WHATEVER, SO SHE FOUND US SOME UNDERPRIVILEGED KIDS TO TUTOR.

MAGIC IS REAL!

REACH for the CLOUDS!! so if you fall you stay on the ground

Library Hours:

YAY

Phonics system invented by Blaise Pascal

"Aliens walk among us" 12...Abe Lincoln

I FOUND A LEAD ONLINE, THOUGH. SUPPOSEDLY MAGICAL DOG COLLAR. IT'S FIFTEEN THOUSAND DOLLARS ON UPPERSTRATA.

OOH!

BUY IT!!

PREMIUM PRICES

CIRCUS

SHOULD WE SPLIT UP? MIGHT GO FASTER.

STRESSED OUT

COMMERCIAL SPACE FOR RENT

RQUE

CIRQUE de SUBURBIA NO REFUNDS

122

123

interesting....

FLIP

ha ha

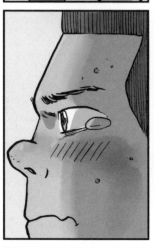

Yikes

...Goblin Boy... haha Ken Stop

TIME! OKAY, WHO'S NEXT?

glance

124

YOU READY TO FLY AROUND AIMLESSLY LOOKING FOR THE *BLUE BANDIT*?

YUP.

MELTON'S VERY OWN CRYPTID. MY LIFE IS AWESOME.

MAYBE WE CAN LOOK FOR THE HINN *AND* VILLAINY AT THE SAME TIME? NO ONE'S HAD ANY LUCK ON PATROL YET.

YEAH! I'M READY FOR WHATEVER LIFE THROWS AT ME!

CHECK OUT WHAT I CAN DO.

;; wobble
wobble

YOU BEEN WORKING ON THAT TRICK?

yeah!

SKITTER

AAHHH!! KILL IT!

LEAVE HIM ALONE, HE'S JUST A FELLOW TRAVELER.

Look at him go!!

126

HAVE YOU SEEN THIS DOG?

DANG, JONAS, THIS FRISBEE IS SITTIN' TIGHT.

HAVE YOU SEEN ME?

THE BLUE BANDIT? I WISH...

whoa

WOW

LET US KNOW IF ANY CRIME NEEDS TO BE FOUGHT!

PLEASE TAKE A FLYER!

SHOO! GO AWAY!

...

LOCAL HEROES

HAVE YOU SEEN ME?
TIPS? CALL

EXCUSE ME, MA'AM—HAVE YOU SEEN THIS DOG?

mrow

hiss

Yay kitty!

here you go!

SOLAR FLARE!

THAT'S NOT GONNA BURN THE KITTEN, IS IT...?

WHAT DO YOU THINK I AM, A SERIAL KILLER?

UHH... THIS ISN'T OUR CAT...

THERE'S NO HINN AND NO CRIME TO FIGHT. MELTON SUCKS.

WE *DID* SAVE ALL THOSE CATS.

Don't even look at them...

weirdos, mommy!

MAYBE WE SHOULD GO BACK TO SPOTS WHERE THE BLUE BANDIT WAS SPOTTED. LIKE THE VACUUM STORE.

BUT I ALREADY LOOKED THERE!

YEAH, BUT HE MIGHT'VE LEFT A CLUE YOU MISSED.

OOH! WAIT!

IT'S A NEGOTIATING TACTIC. DOGS *LOVE* CHEESE.

ALSO I'M GETTING HUNGRY.

FIRE +S WOOD

MELTON EXTR EME

ENTER

ATM

SOFT SERVE ME!

ERMAGHERF!

PARKING FOR Dusty's OLD-FASHIONED VACUUM WAREHOUSE ONLY

ING

THE BLUE BANDIT!

AW... POOR PUP'S HUNGRY...

130

132

COUGH COUGH...
ARE YOU... *COUGH*?

I'M SO
TIRES

Cough
cough
cough

Magic phone,
where are
we?

You are in Newark,
New Jersey.

WE NEED TO GET
THE HINN BACK FROM
NICK. EVERY MINUTE
HE HAS--

wheeze
wheeze

COUGH COUGH

TURN

WE'LL FIGURE
SOMETHING
OUT.

PAT
PAT

KOFF

WHAT IF YOU DRAW A MAGIC-DAMPENING FORCE FIELD GENERATOR?

GET THAT PUPPY INTO A FORCE FIELD AND—

ENJOY RESPONSIBILITY

SPONGES

CHIPS

TWIGS & STIX

MY MOM TOOK MY SKETCHBOOK AWAY.

H₃O Hydrogen Fortified Water

...SHE PROMISED NOT TO USE IT...

IS YOUR MOM **TRUSTWORTHY**?

UH...

XLO Lemon Chamomile Seltzer

SHE COULD TEAR THE **FABRIC** OF **REALITY!** WHY ARE YOU JUST MENTIONING THIS NOW?!

WELCOME TO SKEEZY MART

PLEASE WASH YOUR HANDS

HORN DOG

SORRY

TRA

UH...

Sorry gimme a sec

DOO DOO

Skeezy Mart

MAMA?

NO, I'M FINE. GONNA BE HOME LATE.

YEAH, WITHOUT ME. OKAY.

LOVE YOU TOO. BYE.

SK

94LP Lemon Chamomile Seltzer

138

FOR RENT
MEDICAL OFFICE
MEDICAL LICENSE
MEDICINE
CALL xxx-xxxx

SKEEZY MART

Vesuvio's
FINE DINING

MOBSTERS
EAT FREE!

WE'VE GOTTA TELL EVERYONE ABOUT NICK, AND THE HINN, AND THE SKETCHBOOK—

...SO I THINK MOM'S MAGIC AMULET PROTECTED HER FROM MY MAGICAL MINDWIPE T-SHIRT, AND ONCE SHE REALIZED WHAT I TRIED TO DO—

A T-SHIRT?

NO ONE CAN RESIST FREE T-SHIRTS. I WAS TRYING TO GET UNGROUNDED.

I *ALWAYS* WONDERED WHY THE SCHOOL GAVE OUT T-SHIRTS COMMEMORATING A *LIFE-THREATENING METEOR STRIKE.*

IT WAS *YOU* WHO MINDWIPED EVERYONE AFTER THE GYM ATTACK.

??

...

IS THAT WHY EVERYONE THOUGHT IT WAS A METEOR?

BUT IF WE REMEMBER PRINCE NEPTUNE, DOESN'T THAT MEAN WE WEREN'T MINDWIPED?

DANY...

DANY WOULDN'T MINDWIPE **US**!

...JUST LOOK AT YOUR SHIRT, JOAN!

I SURVIVE MELTON METEOR

WHY WOULD YOU BRAINWASH YOUR **FRIENDS**?

Y-YOU WOULDN'T LISTEN TO ME... IT WAS ALL I COULD THINK OF...

SHAME

SHAME

whyyy

SO, WHAT'S THE BIG NEWS?

boo hoo...

EVERYONE'S MAD AT ME; GO PRETEND TO BE ME AND APOLOGIZE TO THEM...

...

DANY, YOU'RE NOT FOOLING US!

I'M SORRY. I'LL NEVER DO IT AGAIN, I SWEAR.

emerge

140

YOU COULD JUST MINDWIPE US AGAIN AND MAKE US FORGET THIS.

ohh...
whisper

WHEN I SAW HOW NICK TREATED HIS MOM— I DON'T WANT TO BE LIKE HIM. EVER.

UM, SPEAKING OF NICK: HE MAY HAVE THE BLUE BANDIT, BUT I'VE GOT SOMETHING...

IT'S MADE OF DJINN BLOCKS. IT'S SUPPOSED TO HAVE A HANDICAP EFFECT ON MAGIC. I GOT IT ON THE INTERNET.

WOW!

COOL!

IT'S WORTH A SHOT.

...AND THEN KATHLEEN INVITED ME TO THIRSTY THURSDAY. I WAS IN SHOCK.

...SITTING WITH THE COOL KIDS... HAHAHA

...TOOK LONG ENOUGH...

...if Gene could see you now...

STAHHP!

hi

WHY DO YOU SMELL LIKE SMOKE?! DO WE NEED TO HAVE A "TALK"?

I SWEAR TO GOD, MOM, I WAS JUST ADJACENT TO A PILLAR OF BLACK SMOKE. **THAT'S ALL.**

sniff...

TRACE'S HELPING US FIGURE OUT THE PAPERWORK FOR THIS *CASH4LYFE* MESS.

...SHE SAID IT'S ILLEGAL TO TAX US BEFORE WE'VE COLLECTED OUR WINNINGS.

HI, HONEY! LINDA, TELL HER THE NEWS.

I GOT A PROMOTION AT WORK.

THEY PUT ME ON THE HENDERSON PROJECT.

How2.com DECLARING BANKRUPTCY

WOW, CONGRATS, MOM!

IT'S GETTING LATE— LET'S FINISH THIS TOMORROW, OKAY?

WHAT IF WE MOVED AWAY AND STARTED OVER SOMEWHERE ELSE? WOULDN'T THAT BE *FUN*?

HONEY. CHANGING YOUR EXTERIOR CIRCUMSTANCES WON'T CHANGE THE PROBLEMS INSIDE. TRUST ME ON THIS ONE.

THERE'S A SCHOOL DANCE COMING UP. IT'S GONNA BE REALLY LAME AND IN THE SCHOOL PARKING LOT. WE'LL PROBABLY ALL GET RUN OVER BY DRUNK DRIVERS. CAN I GO?

THAT'S FINE WITH ME.

R-REALLY?

I MEAN... I DON'T **MIND** STAYING HOME.

I KNOW.

SO YOU... **WANT** ME TO GO TO THE DANCE?

I NEED TO GO TO THE MALL, ANYWAY. I'LL HELP YOU PICK OUT YOUR DRESS.

THE DANCE IS TOMORROW.

WHY DIDN'T YOU TELL ME SOONER?

(sigh)

BECAUSE I DON'T WANT TO GO? MADISON IS MAKING ME.

I SKIPPED ALL MY SCHOOL DANCES. EVEN PROM.

AND I REGRETTED IT LATER. I DON'T WANT THAT TO HAPPEN TO YOU.

YOU'LL HAVE *FUN.* I PROMISE.

...

...NOW GO TAKE A BATH.

2:10 pm

6m ago

MADISON: DANY!!! Come to the School parking lot NOW! I really need ur help! I'm dying!!!!

MADISON sent you a reminder: "DANCE 2NITE!!" 1:45

ALERT: Sad memes for you!

hm...

SAVE
ME

THIS WOULD BE A LOT EASIER IF WE COULD *FLY.*

HAND ME MORE STREAMERS.

YOUR DAD SEEMED...

DO YOU THINK HE'LL SHOW UP? I TOLD COACH HE'D CHAPERONE. HE PROMISED...

HE'LL BE HERE!

WHAT IF EVERYONE SKIPS THE DANCE? IS THE PARKING LOT LAME?

EVERYONE COOL IS COMING. DON'T WORRY SO MUCH.

CARA! MADISON! WE NEED AN EXTRA SET OF HANDS HERE!

Yeah

2:15

I'm dying!!!

Sending...

OMG I'm so sorry I didn't see this & I'm home already!!! Is everything OK?

LOOK, I'M NOT INTERESTED IN BEING YOUR *SUBSTITUTE DANY* FOREVER.

I HAVE ASPIRATIONS OF MY OWN, YOU KNOW?

I WANNA HIT THE ROAD, JOIN THE CIRCUS, AND LIKE, GO ON SOME CRAZY ADVENTURE.

BECAUSE I'VE GOT NO PAPER TRAIL! I CAN BE ANYONE!

NO ONE WILL LOOK FOR ME! CAN YOU IMAGINE?

WHILE YOU'RE STUCK IN SCHOOL, I CAN BE BUSKING ON STREET CORNERS WITH MY RAGTAG GROUP OF CIRCUS FRIENDS...

...YOU WANT TO LEAVE?

well...

148

I PROMISE YOU, NO MATTER WHAT, I'LL STICK AROUND UNTIL WE'VE BECOME THE COOLEST—

ER, A MODERATELY ACCEPTED INDIVIDUAL.

SO I'LL GO TO THE DANCE. I'LL TRY TO WIN OVER ALL THE RANDOS FOR YOU. DON'T WORRY.

BUT YES. SOMEDAY, I'LL HOP A FREIGHT TRAIN OUT OF THIS PLACE.

SOMEDAY.

WANT ME TO DROP YOU *OFF* RIGHT HERE?

OKAY.

HOW DO I LOOK?

CURTSY

BEAUTIFUL.

SO BEAUTIFUL I *HAVE* TO DOCUMENT IT.

DROP OFF

cheeee...

CHIK

YOUR HAIR, DID YOU DO SOMETHING TO IT?

USUALLY IT HAS SO MUCH VOLUME—

mooOMm!!

FLUFF FLUFF

Bat Bat

I STRAIGHTENED IT!

WHERE'S MADISON? I WANTED TO GET PICTURES OF YOU TWO TOGETHER.

hurr hurr hurr

I THINK WE'RE DOING PICS INSIDE AT THE DANCE.

hang on...

AW...

...WANT ME TO TAKE ONE OF THE TWO OF YOU TOGETHER?

OH! UH...

OLDER SISTER, RIGHT? NO WAY YOU'RE *HER* MOM.

NO THANKS, I'M FINE.

151

155

DON'T CALL ME BACK UNTIL YOU'VE GOT SOME GOOD NEWS! I'M AT MY DAUGHTER'S-- YEAH-- *FIX IT!*

TURN

EUGENE. EUGENE MCCOY.

ARE YOU CARA'S FATHER?

YOU KNOW MY GIRL?

...CARA'S JUST *WONDERFUL.*

SHE'S GOOD FRIENDS WITH OUR MADISON.

MADISON! MADISON'S A REAL SPITFIRE. SHE'S GREAT.

HOLD ON, I GOTTA TAKE THIS—

TALK TO ME, KENNETH...

The Blue Bandit?

Dude...

4SALE: choco LAST CHANCE 50 cents

PAY HERE

IS THAT NICK MALONEY?

THE MEAN KID? IS HE HERE? WHAT DOES HE LOOK LIKE?

...HE'S GOT MAGIC, LEAH! HE MADE HIMSELF... DIFFERENT...

HE NORMALLY LOOKS LIKE AN EVIL LITTLE TROLL. THAT'S HIM OVER THERE.

where?

TIPPYTOE

HIM?!

YEAH.

whisper whisper

LITTLE NICKY IS A BULLY?!

157

HUH? YOU **KNOW** HIM?

YES, A LITTLE. HE GOES TO MY CHURCH.

YOU CALL HIM "LITTLE NICKY"?!

heh heh

THAT'S WHAT **EVERYONE** CALLS HIM. I DIDN'T EVEN KNOW HE **HAD** A LAST NAME.

THOUGH I GUESS HE'S... BIG NICKY NOW...

creepy...

BRB

I CAN'T BELIEVE **LITTLE NICKY** IS YOUR BULLY.

GUYS!

I JUST SAW NICK MALONEY! HE BROUGHT THE BLUE BANDIT!

CARA. YOU'RE IN LOVE WITH ME. ASK ME TO DANCE.

Uh...

NICK! I'M DESPERATELY IN LOVE WITH YOU! DANCE WITH ME!

how—?

CARA!

LEAVE HER ALONE!

OH, LOOK. IT'S THE *SOLAR GEEKS.*

WHAT...
JUST...

YOU'LL
PAY—

MADISON,
GO CLIMB
A TREE.

YOU THINK
YOU'RE *POWERFUL*.
YOU'RE *NOTHING*
NEXT TO DANY.

NEXT TO
ALL OF US.

heh

IF YOU'RE
SO POWERFUL,
WHY DON'T YOU
COME DOWN FROM
THE TREE?

LEAVE HER
ALONE!

DANIEL THE MANIEL. ASK ME TO DANCE.

GRRR...

murph murph murph.

I DIDN'T CATCH THAT.

Hance... Hith....

CLENCH

DANCE WITH ME!

NICK... YOU CAN'T... DO THIS...

YES I CAN. I CAN DO WHATEVER I *DREAM*.

Sneak

ALERT! ALERT! ALRIGHT ALREADY!!

EMERGE

GASP

ALERT: Pikkimal Life-Form TERMINATED

N-no!!! CLONEY!!!

THIS CAN'T BE HAPPENING...

CLÖN LABS

EXIT

BZZT

BRING HER BACK!

HOW DID YOU—

UNDO IT! PLEASE!

I... I DON'T KNOW HOW...

STUPID DOG...

165

BY THE RAYS OF THE SUN, **TRANSFORM!**

CLÖN LABS

TRANSFORM

POSE!

FIVE AGAINST ONE? TCH, **THAT'S** FAIR!

AXEL, COME **HERE**! WHAT ARE YOU DOING?!

JOAN— THE COLLAR! TAKE IT!

you didn't mean it...

ruf?

huff huff

C'MON, WHAT THE HECK?!

SORRY...

UGH! THIS WASN'T SUPPOSED TO HAPPEN! AXEL!

COME **HERE!** WHY AREN'T YOU LISTENING?

GOT IT! THE COLLAR'S WORKING!

CLICK

GET AWAY FROM THEM! STUPID DOG!!

GASP

KICK

YELP!!

169

FWOOOO

DAD?

CREE CREEK chkchkchk

AXEL, CALM DOWN. THE COLLAR'S GONE.

Bruff

YOU'RE GONNA BE GOOD, RIGHT?

AXEL, I NEED TO BE STRONG. BIG AND STRONG AND POWERFUL, OKAY?

LICK

TAKE A LOOK AT WHAT YOU'RE DOING, NICK.

WHAT ARE YOU GONNA DO ABOUT IT? YOU'RE NO MATCH FOR ME.

MAYBE YOU'RE RIGHT.

BUT DO WE REALLY HAVE TO FIGHT? MAYBE WE SHOULD JUST TAKE A STEP BACK AND...

meow

SAVE ME

AVE ELTON

munch munch

WHAT'S YOUR REAL NAME, BABY? IS IT REALLY AXEL?

wag

EVERYONE, LOOK! SHE LIKES CHOCOLATE! AWW!

ISN'T CHOCOLATE POISON FOR DOGS?

hnn...

PENELOPE?

AXEL! NO!! DROP IT!

Hnnk! Hnnk!

...THAT'S NOT GOING TO HAPPEN.

MRS. MARKS!

JUST TAKE YOUR DOG AND *GO.*

YOU, DANY?

I DON'T EVEN *KNOW* WHAT TO DO WITH YOU.

MAGIC IS REAL?

I'LL TALK TO YOU *LATER.*

BUT *YOU,* NICK?

YOU'RE *SUSPENDED INDEFINITELY.* WE'RE GOING TO HAVE A CHAT IN MY OFFICE. COME WITH ME.

I SUGGEST YOU FIND THE DOG ANOTHER HOME.

I'LL TAKE HER! *DIBS!*

185

AM I A MAN WHO DREAMED I WAS A SQUIRREL? OR AM I A SQUIRREL WHO DREAMS I AM A MAN?

REX? SKYE? ...CAN WE KEEP HER?

MADISON...

PLEASE, BE REALISTIC.

PLEASE?

PLEEEEASE?

REX AND I HAVE OUR HANDS FULL WITH YOU KIDS! WE CAN'T JUST ADOPT A *MAGICAL DOG!*

BUT... *MAYBE...* WE CAN TALK ABOUT ADOPTING A NICE STRAY FROM THE POUND.

...BUT WHERE WILL PENELOPE GO?

I'LL TAKE HER. IT'S MY MESS TO CLEAN UP.

SEE?

...

C'MON, PUP!

MAGIC IS REAL!! MY LIFE IS A LIE!!!

WHOAAAOOH

do you believe in magic? In a young dog's bark

...I'LL BE RIGHT BACK.

187

MAGIC IS REAL, MAGIC IS REAL, SING IT WITH ME!

MAGIC IS REAL, MAGIC IS REAL...

FOONP

MAGIC IS REAL, MAGIC IS REAL...

I danced my ARFS AWAY at the SAVE MELTON DANCEATHON

ARE THOSE FREE T-SHIRTS? NICE!

HEY!!

WHOA...

I danced cares aw

SOLAR FLARE!

FSHHH

HEY! NOT COOL!

HMM...

THERE'S JUST ENOUGH POWDER TO DO THE JOB.

FLAP FLAP

...I GUESS I *COULD* FIX THE SCHOOL MYSELF.

LEAVE IT! NOT FOOD!

SNIF SNIF

SHAKE

I THOUGHT SHE COULD USE SOME PEACE AND QUIET.

SO...

...ARE YOU GONNA BRING BACK CLONEY?

...I CAN'T.

SHE SHOULDN'T HAVE EXISTED IN THE FIRST PLACE. BUT ALSO—

I'D BRING YOU BACK IF ANYTHING HAPPENED TO YOU.

WELL, NOTHING'S GONNA HAPPEN TO ME! SHEESH.

WHAT ARE YOU GONNA DO WITH PENELOPE?

DOG MODE

UPDATING.....

type type

YOU'RE SAYING I CAN KEEP THE PIKKIBALL?

WELL, IT'S PERFECT FOR PENELOPE.

AND WITH... CLONEY GONE...

...IT'S LIKE SHE NEVER EXISTED.

I NEVER WANTED TO HURT ANYONE AT ALL. YOU KNOW THAT, RIGHT, MADISON?

OF COURSE
I DO.

LET'S GET
BACK TO
THE DANCE.

BUT
I'M NOT
READY...

THE PARTY'S
NOT GONNA WAIT
FOR YOU!

EXIT

C'MON! You'll have fun!

CHEER!

I DON'T CARE WHAT I SAID BEFORE! I TAKE IT BACK.

autographs

YOU'RE COOL IN MY BOOK, DANY.

WOO!

MAGIC IS REAL!

REALLY?

...

DANCEY DANCE

YOU SAVED MY DAD'S LIFE. YEAH, DORK.

YOU'RE COOL NOW.

pat pat

Clancy... we did it...

it's PENELOPE'S PUPPY COMICS CORNER!

"Ruff."

Here is a selection of my earthly adventures.

I CAME BACK EVENTUALLY

ALL RIGHT, PENELOPE, BACK IN YOUR BALL.

PIKKIBALL, GO!

!!

TOSS

SCAMPER

PENELOPE! NO!

DOG IS MY CAR PILOT

I WISH TO BE THE COOLEST BOY AT THE DANCE!

BUT I'M NOT 16! WHO'S GOING TO DRIVE—

FWOO FWOOSH

Ruff.

!!

Get in.